Return of the Pumpkin Head

by Jenny Miglis

illustrated by
Stephen Destefano
and Mike Giles

Simon Spotlight/Nickelodeon
New York London Toronto Sydney Singapore

To my dad, the original pumpkin head.—JM

Based on the TV series *The Adventures of Jimmy Neutron, Boy Genius*™ as seen on Nickelodeon®

SIMON SPOTLIGHT
An imprint of Simon & Schuster Children's Publishing Division
1230 Avenue of the Americas, New York, NY 10020
Copyright © 2003 Viacom International Inc. All rights reserved. NICKELODEON,
The Adventures of Jimmy Neutron, Boy Genius, and all related titles, logos, and
characters are trademarks of Viacom International Inc. All rights reserved,
including the right of reproduction in whole or in part in any form.
SIMON SPOTLIGHT and colophon are registered trademarks of Simon & Schuster.
Manufactured in the United States of America
10 9 8 7 6 5 4 3 2
ISBN 0-689-85847-7

It was a dark and stormy Halloween night," Jimmy Neutron began an old Retroville ghost story, "and the mean farmer who lived in the house next to the pumpkin patch caught some kids stealing his pumpkins. He yelled at them and chased them away. Later that night one of the kids cast a spell on the angry farmer. The next morning the farmer awoke to find that he had grown a big, round pumpkin for a head! Legend has it that the ghost of the farmer haunts the pumpkin patch every Halloween . . . seeking revenge . . . searching for children to turn into . . . PUMPKIN HEADS!"

Carl burst through the flaps of the tent in Jimmy Neutron's backyard.

"I don't like that scary stuff, Jimmy!" cried Carl.

"You know what's scary?" said Sheen. "I bet that old abandoned house next to the pumpkin patch is *really* scary." He exchanged a knowing glance with Jimmy. "It would be the perfect place for the ultimate haunted house!"

The next morning the boys got to work on the haunted house.

First they rigged the condensation machine to the roof. A rain cloud formed above the house while lightning cracked and thunder boomed.

Then they installed the automatic door opener with a pop-up skeleton.

Robotic tarantulas scurried across the metallic cobwebs they had strung from the ceiling.

Goddard emitted a high-pitched howl heard only by dogs. The neighborhood erupted in menacing barks.

Then Jimmy poured a bag of dry ice onto the ground. "Now I will create a disorienting fog. A shameless second-grade level use of science, but effective nonetheless," he said. "Gentlemen, meet my *monster*piece. . . ."

A large lumbering figure emerged from the fog. It had an abnormally large, misshapen head.

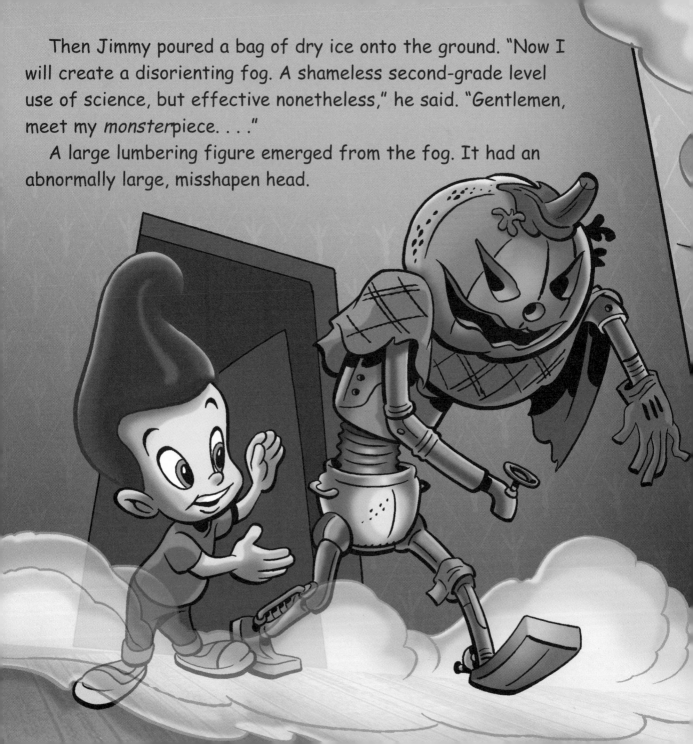

"It's, it's, it's . . . the Pumpkin Head!" cried Carl as he cowered behind Sheen.

"Don't worry, Carl. It's just my remote-controlled version," said Jimmy, marveling at his workmanship. "It's genius!" He threw his head back and chortled like a mad scientist.

Back in town Cindy and Libby were working on their Halloween costumes. "Don't look now," said Cindy. "But here come the fright-night nerds."

Jimmy handed the girls two invitations. "We're throwing a party at the pumpkin patch," he said.

"Uh, a perfectly harmless Halloween party, of course," Carl chimed in. Nick Dean skidded to a stop on his skateboard. "Did you say somethin' about *throwing pumpkins*, Nerdtron? I am so there!"

Later that afternoon Jimmy, Carl, and Sheen were putting the finishing touches on the haunted house.

"Jimmy, would you please stop the robotic tarantulas from attacking me?" Carl pleaded.

"Huh? Oh, there must be a glitch in the program. I'll fix it in a minute," Jimmy replied. *Whooh! Whooooh!* "Carl, stop whining," said Jimmy. "I said I'd get to it in a minute."

"I'm over here, Jimmy!" Carl called from across the room.

The hairs on Jimmy's neck stood up. "Something strange is going on here," he said. "Goddard, scan for supernatural life forms!"

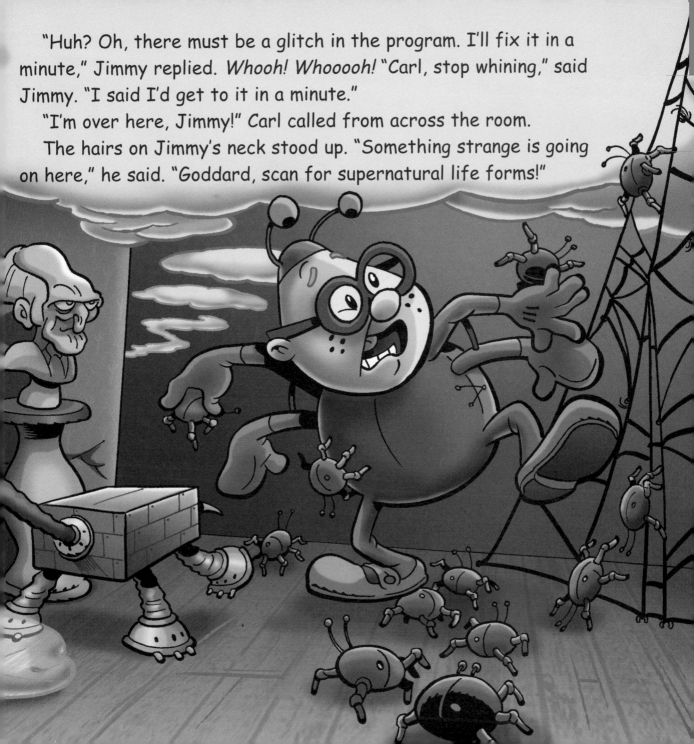

Beep, beep, beeeeep! Goddard's radar detected something.

"Pukin' pluto!" said Jimmy. "I think we have a ghost on our hands!"

"W-W-What do we do?" asked Carl.

"Let's call UltraLord!" Sheen suggested. "Master of the Universe, ghost slayer extraordinaire . . ."

"Think, think, think," Jimmy said to himself. But his thoughts were interrupted by something that caught his eye outside.

A figure was wading through the tangled vines in the pumpkin patch. It looked just like Jimmy's Pumpkin Head invention.

"Sheen, I told you not to use the remote control on the Pumpkin Head until everyone gets here," Jimmy scolded.

"I didn't, Jimmy," said Sheen from behind. "I was just making him into Ultra-Pumpkin Head."

Jimmy spun around.

"If the Pumpkin Head is in here, then who—or *what*—is that?" Carl pointed outside.

"Uh, there's a perfectly rational explanation," said Jimmy. "It's, um, our collective subconscious playing tricks on us. Our young, impressionable brains have been scarred by too many scary movies. We're just imagining things. . . ."

Carl began to tremble. "I don't like to be the bearer of bad news, but the *imaginary* Pumpkin Head is coming closer and closer!" he squealed.

"It's heading toward the side door," said Jimmy. "Let's make a run for the front door. On three. One . . ."

But before Jimmy could finish the count, the boys were gone.
Carl flung the front door open. "AHHHHH!" he screamed.
Three hideous Pumpkin Heads were blocking his way.

Goddard bolted through the doorway, knocking the monsters to the ground.
The pumpkin head on the first monster rolled off, revealing Cindy Vortex.
"Uh, trick-or-treat!" Cindy said with a giggle.
Libby and Nick removed their pumpkin heads, laughing.

Just then another pumpkin-headed monster rounded the corner, making horrible moaning sounds. *Whooh! Whooooh!*

Cindy looked at Libby, shocked. "W-W-Who's that?" she cried. As the huge monster lurched toward them she let out a piercing scream.

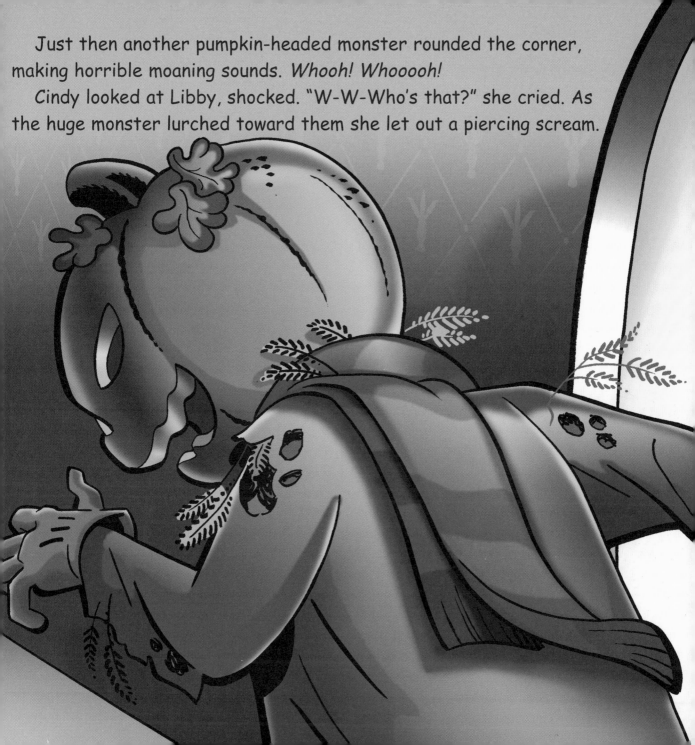

"Stop screaming!" the monster cried. "I have a terrible headache!" The monster took the pumpkin off of his head, revealing the farmer underneath. "Whew! That thing is heavy. Didn't mean to scare you kids . . . well, actually, I guess I did. I was just acting as a scarecrow—or scare*kid*—for my pumpkin patch. You see, I spend the winters in Florida, and I've got to do something to keep the kids from messing up my pumpkin patch every Halloween."

"You mean you made up the story of the Pumpkin Head?" asked Carl in disbelief.

"'Fraid so," the farmer replied. "But now that the cat's outta the bag, I suppose I'll have to take up orange groves in Florida instead."

"Well, that might not be necessary," said Jimmy. "I think we can keep your legend alive for you."

Jimmy took out his remote control and pressed a button. But it got stuck. The Pumpkin Head zoomed into the house and barreled into the farmer, knocking the pumpkin right onto Jimmy's head.

Cindy howled with laughter. "Look, it's Jimmy Pumpkin Head!" she crowed.

"Here we go again," Jimmy sighed. "It's going to be a long year until next Halloween."